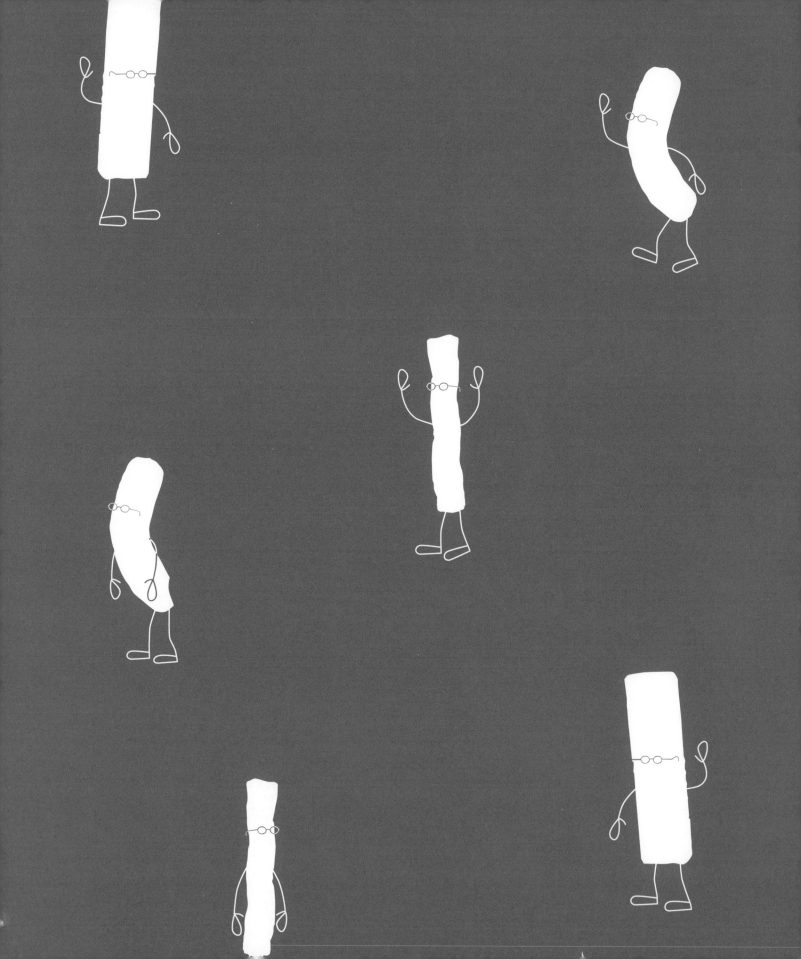

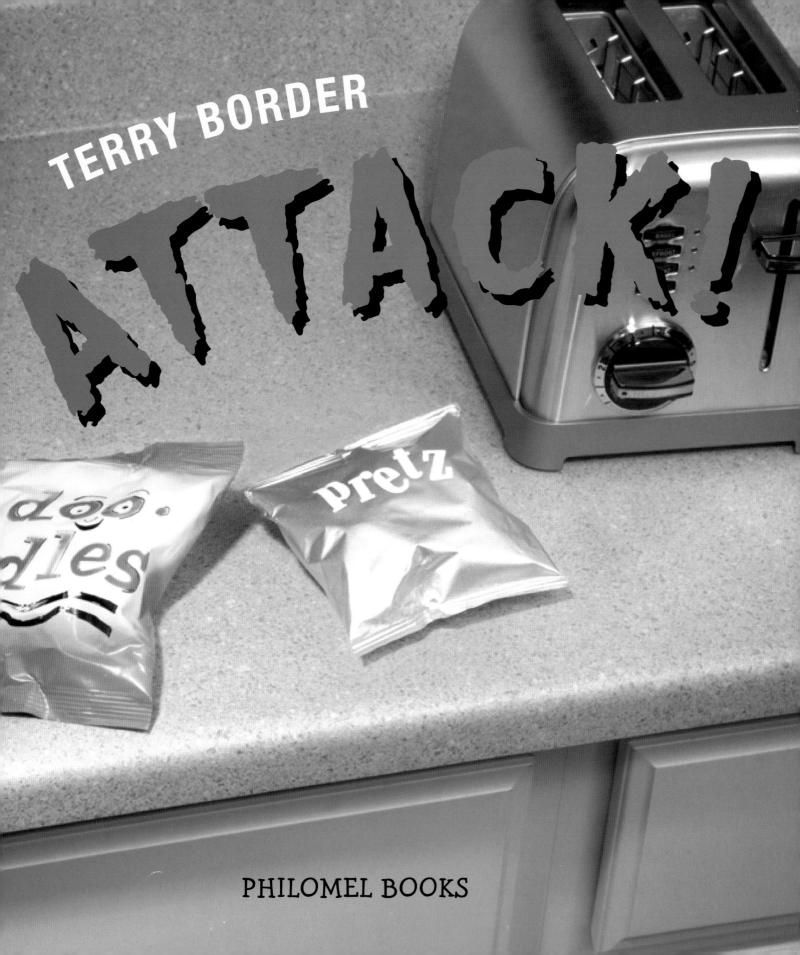

PHILOMEL BOOKS

An imprint of Penguin Random House LLC
New York

First published in the United States of America by Philomel Books, an imprint of Penguin Random House LLC, 2019

Library of Congress Cataloging-in-Publication Data
Names: Border, Terry, 1965- author, illustrator. Title: Snack attack! / Terry Border.
Description: [New York] : Philomel Books, 2019. | Summary: Although warned of the dangers lurking outside their packages, Cookie, Pretzel, and Cheese Doodle venture into the kitchen for fun but soon discover that Monster Kids are real. Identifiers: LCCN 2019018129| ISBN 9781524740115 (hardback) | ISBN 9781524740146 (e-book) | ISBN 9781524740078 (e-book) Subjects: | CYAC: Snack foods—Fiction. | Adventure and adventurers—Fiction. | Humorous stories. | BISAC: JUVENILE FICTION / Humorous Stories. | JUVENILE FICTION / Cooking & Food. | JUVENILE FICTION / Horror & Ghost Stories. Classification: LCC PZ7.B64832 Sn 2019 | DDC [E]—dc23 LC record available at https://lccn.loc.gov/2019018129

Visit us online at penguinrandomhouse.com

Manufactured in China
ISBN 9781524740115
10 9 8 7 6 5 4 3 2 1

Edited by Jill Santopolo.
Design by Angelie Yap and Ellice M. Lee.
Text set in Hank BT.
The art was done by manipulating and photographing three-dimensional objects.

For my Team Zissou

One afternoon, a cheese doodle, a pretzel stick, and a cookie all escaped from their packages, even though they had been warned about the outside world.

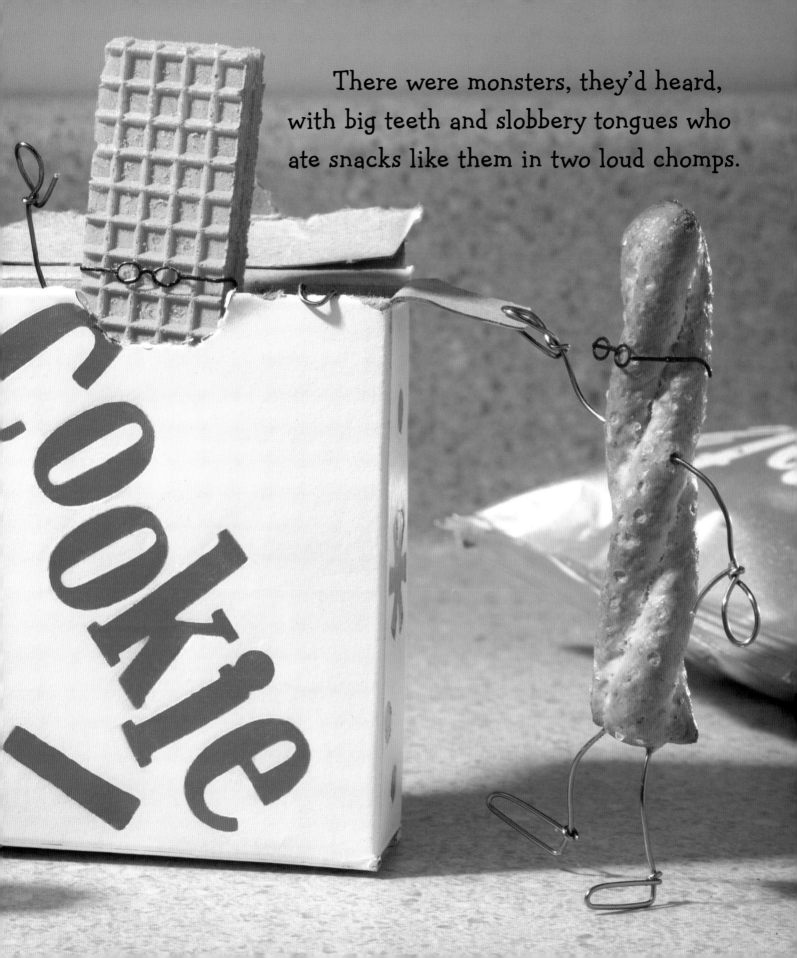

There were monsters, they'd heard, with big teeth and slobbery tongues who ate snacks like them in two loud chomps.

But wherever they were seemed fun, not dangerous.

They even went boating on a pond.

Then they found the note.

Hi Kiddo,

I hope you had a good day at school. I had to go out, so I left you some snacks because I'll be late.

Love
Mom

"Oh no! She means us!" cried Cookie, who was a very smart cookie.

Pretzel and Cheese Doodle asked what a kid was.

"A kid is a kind of monster," said Cookie. "Like the ones we've been warned about. They're giants! A Monster Kid can hold all three of us in one of their humongous, dirty hands! They can squash us to bits!"

"Yikes!" said Pretzel.

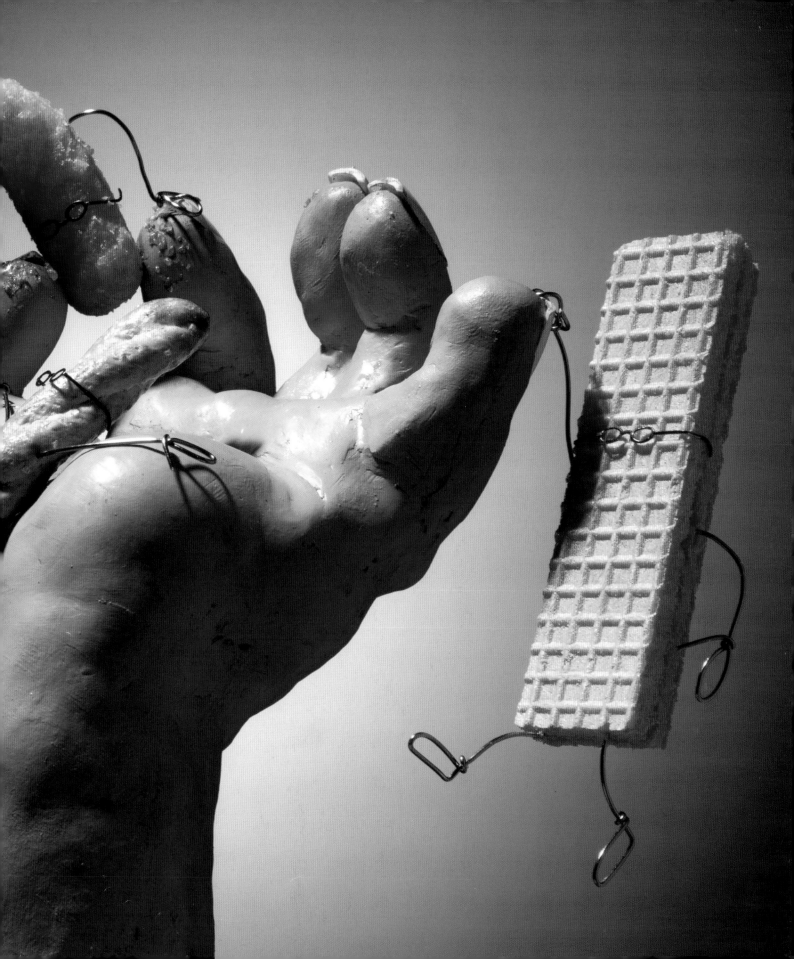

"And that's not the worst part," said Cookie. "They can crack us in half! Dunk us in milk!" She shuddered.

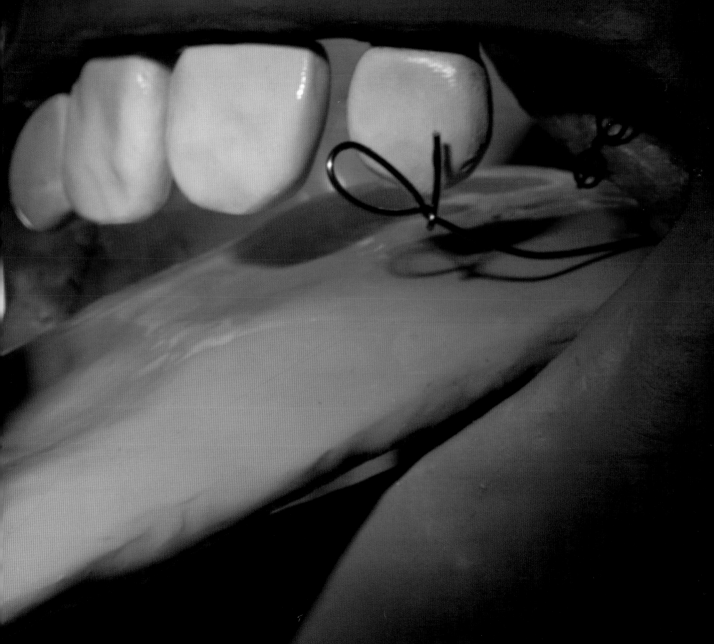

"There's even more!" said Cookie. "They can swallow us all in one monstrous gulp."

"I feel faint!" said Pretzel. "We have to come up with a plan, and quick."

Cheese Doodle had heard about a thing called the five-second rule, where monsters won't eat food if it has been on the floor for longer than five seconds. "Let's roll on the floor for six seconds and make the kid not want to eat us!" he said.

"Nope," said Cookie. "That only works with Monster Moms. Not Monster Kids."

Cheese Doodle came up with another idea. Maybe they could hide!

But after they found a good hiding place, "Ouchy-ouch-OUCH!" yelled Cheese Doodle.

"Oh no!" said Pretzel, "Cheese Doodle got too close to the cheese grater."

"I don't feel greater," cried Cheese Doodle. "It's really a cheese worser!"

Cheese Doodle got one last idea.

His best one yet.

He turned over the note and wrote on the other side.

DEAR KID,
Please drink some water and eat NOTHING ELSE.

From your loving Momma

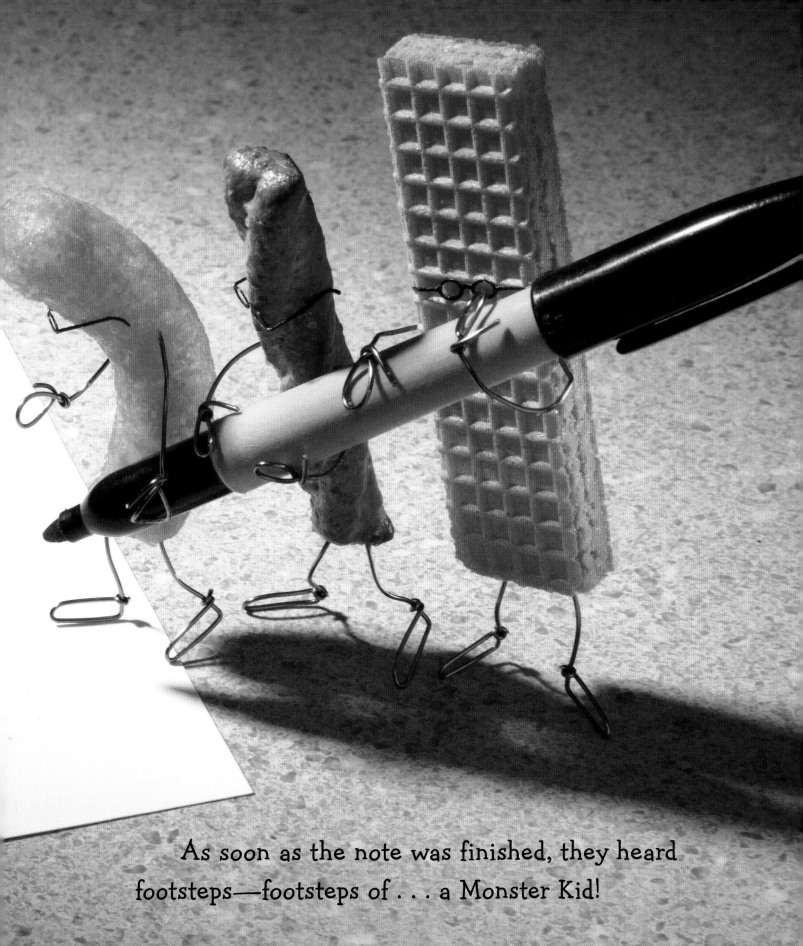

As soon as the note was finished, they heard footsteps—footsteps of . . . a Monster Kid!

The snacks closed their eyes and tried
their best not to shake from fear.

While the Monster Kid read the note, Cheese Doodle took a quick peek and was quite surprised.

Pretzel peeked too. She couldn't believe what she saw! Although the Monster Kid was a giant, it didn't look like a monster at all!

The Monster Kid got some water from the sink and took a nice long sip.

"My plan worked!" said Cheese Doodle once the kid had left. "What a relief!"

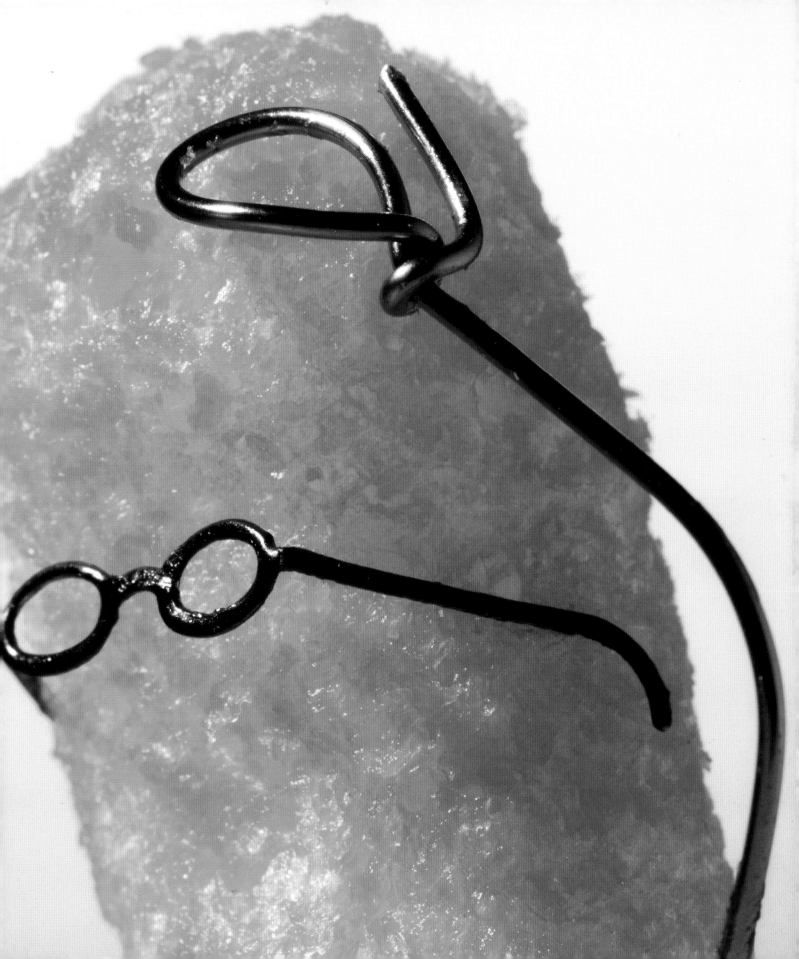

"It didn't seem unhappy about that nice glass of water," said Pretzel. "Maybe we can be friends with the Monster Kid!"

"I think we can!" said Cheese Doodle. "How about you, Cookie? Hey, Cookie, where are you?"